D1475163

For my grandfather Vernon, who enjoyed reading my
stories when I was a child.

Donated by author

GETS HER FEELINGS OUT

By: Tabitha M. Johnson, M.A., LMFT

Illustrated By: Julius I. Johnson

I used to eat my feelings

I used to stuff them down

Now I know that it's okay

To sometimes wear a frown

I used to hide my feelings

And felt such guilt and shame

Worried about being exposed

In fear of being blamed

I used to stuff my mouth with food

Which I didn't really taste

Afterwards I felt horrible

My parents, I couldn't face

This became my daily thing

As I continued to age

Overeating hurt my body

I kept my feelings in a cage

The feelings that I may have

Are happy, mad, sad or scared

I didn't want to tell anyone

Because I didn't think they cared

I am learning to share my feelings

With someone who I trust

I don't have to stuff my feelings down

But talk it out I must

When I feel mad or when I'm sad

I can breathe in deep

I can write in my journal

Or even go to sleep

I can move my body

Or even go out to play

It's okay to feel my feelings

Each and every day

Sometimes I may cry

Sometimes I may shout

I now know that I must

Get my feelings out

CRY

SHOUT FEELINGS OUT

FEELINGS

So if you feel mad or even sad

It really is okay

Feelings come and feelings go

Every single day

Dealing with your feelings

Will help you to relate

With others in this world

No need to isolate

You can share your feelings

Just like I did too

Your feelings are necessary

And a part of you

Tabitha M. Johnson, M.A., LMFT, is a licensed marriage and family therapist and certified health coach who resides in Henderson, NV. She began her clinical career working with children. She continues to work with people of all ages and specializes in trauma.

She lives with her husband and two children. She enjoys being with her family and likes to run and rhyme in her spare time.

The illustrator of this book, Julius I. Johnson, is the son of Tabitha Johnson. He enjoys being creative with both drawing and building.